Keeping Unusual Pets

RATS

June McNicholas

Heinemann Library
Chicago, Illinois

Customer Service 888-454-2279
Visit our website at www.heinemannlibrary.com

Designed by Celia Floyd
Originated by Dot Gradiations Limited
Printed in China

07 06 05 04
10 9 8 7 6 5 4 3

Library of Congress Cataloging-in-Publication Data
McNicholas, June, 1956-
  Rats / June McNicholas.
      p. cm. -- (Keeping unusual pets)
Summary: Describes how to select a pet rat, what to feed it, and when to take it to the vet, as well as how to keep a pet scrapbook.
Includes bibliographical references (p.   ).
  ISBN 1-40340-283-3
  1. Rats as pets--Juvenile literature. [1. Rats as pets. 2. Pets.] I.
Title. II. Series.
  SF459.R3 M36 2002
  636.9'352--dc21

                        2002003164

Acknowledgments
The author and publisher are grateful to the following for permission to reproduce copyright material: pp. 4, 10, 13 Science Photo Library; pp. 5 (top), 5 (bottom), 8 (top), 8 (bottom), 9 (top), 9 (bottom), 11 (top), 11 (bottom), 12, 14, 15, 18 (top), 18 (bottom), 19 (top), 19 (bottom), 20 (top), 21, 22, 23 (top), 23 (bottom), 24, 25 (top), 25 (bottom), 26 (top), 26 (bottom), 27, 28, 29 (left), 29 (right), 31 (top), 31 (bottom), 33 (top), 33 (bottom), 35 (top), 35 (bottom), 37 (top), 40, 44 (top), 44 (bottom) Gareth Boden; pp. 6, 16, 17 (top), 17 (bottom), 30, 32 (top), 32 (bottom), 34, 36, 37 (bottom), 38, 41, 45 (top), 45 (bottom) Tudor Photography; p. 7 (top) Bruce Coleman Collection/Jane Burton; p. 7 (bottom) NHPA/Stephen Dalton; p. 20 (bottom) Ardea/Johan De Meester; p. 39 NHPA/Daniel Heuclin; p. 42 Bruce Coleman Collection/Andrew Purcell; p. 43 Maria Joannou.

Cover photograph reproduced with permission of NHPA/Daniel Heuclin.

Special thanks to Kathy Gowenlock and family, and the staff of "Happy Pets" in Droitwich Spa.

Every effort has been made to contact copyright holders of any material reproduced in this book. Any omissions will be rectified in subsequent printings if notice is given to the publisher.

Some words are shown in bold, **like this.** You can find out what they mean by looking in the glossary.

Contents

What Is a Rat?

Most people think of rats as nasty, wild animals that live in sewers and spread diseases. So do not be surprised if people ask you how you could possibly want to keep a rat as a pet!

But are pet rats really so horrible? The answer is, not at all. Pet rats are not the same as wild rats that **scavenge,** or hunt, for food in trash cans or sewers. They have been **domesticated** for many years so they now make excellent and friendly pets.

Wild rats often live on food found in trash cans. They survive by eating anything they can find.

4

Rats in history

Pet rats have a history that goes back hundreds of years. Grand ladies of fashion in the 1800s kept attractive, colored, rats as pets. These were probably just unusually colored wild rats caught by rat catchers. But people came to realize that rats could make affectionate, intelligent pets.

Famous rats

One of the most famous pet rats was a white rat named Sammy. Sammy belonged to Beatrix Potter, the author of the Peter Rabbit stories.

Many people think that rats are the best small pets for adults and children.

Need to know

- Wild rats are classified as **vermin,** or **pests.** It is **illegal** to keep vermin, so you must not take rats from the wild.
- Domesticated rats should not be allowed to **breed** with wild rats or be released into the wild.
- Having a pet is a big responsibility. You should always talk to an adult before bringing an animal home.
- Most countries have laws protecting animals. It is your responsibility to make sure your rats are healthy and well cared for. Always take your pets to the vet if they are ill or have been injured.

Rat Facts

Rats are **mammals.** This means they are **warm-blooded** creatures that give birth to their young and feed their babies with milk. They are members of the **rodent** family, which includes mice, rabbits, guinea pigs, hamsters, and gerbils. In fact, quite a lot of small pets are rodents. All rodents have long teeth for gnawing. A rat's teeth grow throughout its life, so rats need to gnaw to keep their teeth short. If their teeth grow too long, they can die of starvation because they cannot eat properly.

Rats will chew on anything within their reach. Give them chew sticks or blocks of wood to gnaw.

Did you know?

- Rats live for two to three years.
- Male rats are called **bucks** and female rats are called **does.**
- Young rats are called **kittens** and also, occasionally, "pups."
- Male rats can weigh up to 24 ounces (680 grams).
- Female rats weigh between 7 to 17 ounces (200 to 480 grams).
- A rat's tail may be as long as its body.

Rat babies

Rats **mature,** or grow up, very quickly and can have babies of their own when they are only two or three months old. This is one reason why rats can be such **pests** in the wild. Rats have lots of babies in a **litter.** They can have several litters in a year, by which time the babies will have grown up enough to have babies of their own!

Rats use their long tails to help them keep their balance.

Baby rats are called kittens. When they are first born, they have no hair on their bodies and they cannot see.

Clever climbers

Rats are fast-moving, **agile** creatures that are good at climbing. They are very intelligent and are good at solving problems. You can teach a rat to run through a maze to its food and it will remember which route is the quickest. Their intelligence is another reason why rats are pests in the wild— they can find food easily and escape from humans and their traps. But this is also what makes rats very good pets.

Different colors

Pet rats come in lots of different colors. Colors for rats include white, cinnamon (reddish-brown), champagne (cream), chocolate (dark brown), and blue (smoky gray-blue). Rats of specific colors are grouped into types and are often called **fancy rats.** There are also rats that do not belong to a particular type, but they still look pretty and make good pets.

This picture shows a chocolate hooded rat (left) and a cinnamon hooded rat (right).

These rats are a silverthorn (left) and a chocolate rat (right).

A wide choice

There are lots of different types of fancy rats to choose from. A good way to find out more about these varieties is to get in touch with a rat society. You can find details about these in your local phone book or on the Internet. You could also contact your local rat club, visit some rat shows, or talk to rat owners. You will soon find out that rats make excellent pets and that they are nothing like their wild cousins.

The rat above is a mink rat with several different colors.

This picture shows a Berkshire rat (top) and a hooded rat (bottom).

Are Rats For You?

Some people may tell you that rats make the best small pets of all because they are so intelligent and friendly. They might even think that they are more fun to keep than cats or dogs.

As with all pets, there are good and bad things about owning rats. Here are some of the good points and not-so-good points.

Rat good points

- Rats are intelligent. They recognize their owners and love human company.
- Rats will quickly learn your routine. You may find them waiting at the front of their cage when it is time for them to be taken out.
- Rats are not truly **nocturnal,** so they are happy to be up and active when you are.
- Rats are not expensive to buy or to feed.
- Above all, rats have character. They have big personalities in small bodies. This makes them real friends—some are more like little dogs or cats!

Your rats will love to sit on your shoulder. They will probably play with your hair and might even lick your face!

Rat not-so-good points

- A rat can bite hard if it is hurt or frightened.
- Rats will chew absolutely anything they can reach.
- Some **bucks** like to mark places where they have been with a few drops of **urine**. This does not smell, but it can be offensive to some people.
- Sadly, rats do not live long. Most of them only live for about 24 to 30 months.

Yes or no?

So, are rats for you? Having rats for pets means giving them food and water every day, cleaning out their cage every week, and giving them lots of attention. Are you really sure that you are prepared to do all these things, even when you are in a hurry or want to do something else? If the answer is yes, then you could be ready to begin keeping rats as pets. This hobby could last for many years—or even for the rest of your life!

When your rats see you coming, they will run to the front of their cage—all ready to play with you!

Rats are very friendly and trusting. Once your pets have become used to you, they will be happy to sit in your hands.

11

Choosing Your Rats

There are lots of things to think about when you are choosing a rat. Always take an adult with you to help you choose your pet. If possible, ask an experienced rat owner to come along too and give you advice.

One or more?

Rats like the company of other rats. It is perfectly fine to keep a single rat, but you will have to give your pet a lot of time and attention. A lonely rat will probably be very unhappy.

It is much better to keep two rats instead of just one. They will be just as friendly with you, but they will also have each other for company when you are busy. Try to choose two rats of the same age who are already used to each other. Best of all, choose two sisters or two brothers.

Rats are naturally gregarious. That means they enjoy the company of other rats.

Buck or doe?

Usually, **bucks** are bigger than **does.** Bucks are also lazier, so they are probably the best choice if you want a pet that will sit quietly on your lap. The one drawback with bucks is that some of them like to mark the places they have been with a few drops of **urine.** This is a scent mark to let other rats know that your rat is around. We cannot smell it, but other rats can. It is less of a problem than it sounds, but some people do not like the idea very much.

Does are usually more lively and playful than bucks. Most does do not mark places with urine, but a few of them do it just as much as bucks.

Top tips

- If you decide to keep more than one rat, make sure that all your rats are the same sex. If they are not, you could end up with far more pets than you planned for!
- Both bucks and does make equally good pets, so the choice is up to you.
- Try to visit some rat owners and rat shows to get to know a few bucks and does before you decide which will suit you best.

If you have two rats, they will keep each other company when you are not around.

What age?

It is best to choose pet rats that are about eight weeks old. Older rats take longer to get used to their human owners and rats under six weeks are too young to leave their mothers. Unfortunately, many pet store owners will not know exactly how old their rats are, or even what sex they are. Try to take an experienced rat owner with you who may be able to help.

Top tip

Never buy a rat if it has a runny nose or eyes, or if it is sneezing and seems sick.

These young rats look healthy and **alert**, with bright eyes and shiny coats. They would make excellent pets.

What to look for

There are a few basic things to look for when you are choosing rats.

- The rats should be living in clean surroundings.
- They should have bright eyes, clean ears, and a clean tail.
- Their coats should be soft, with no bald patches.
- They should be interested in you and not seem to be nervous.

Your local pet store should have plenty of rats to choose from. Take some time to get to know the rats before choosing one to be your pet.

Top tip

If you are choosing a **doe,** make sure she has been separated from male rats since she was eight weeks old. Otherwise, she could be pregnant. It is unfair for an animal so young to **breed** when she is no more than a baby herself. She still has a lot of growing up to do.

What Do I Need?

Rats can be kept in cages or tanks, but the most important thing is to give your pets plenty of room. Rats are active, playful creatures and they will make good use of whatever space you provide.

Choosing a cage

Most people keep their pet rats in a cage. A cage measuring about 24 × 16 × 16 inches (60 × 40 × 40 cm) is about right for a pair of rats, but try to get a bigger one if you can.

Many pet stores have cages made just for rats. Look for one that is roomy and easy to clean. Cages with metal bars and a plastic tray on the bottom are simple to keep clean. Doors and cage panels need to be secure enough to prevent the rat from escaping, so test them carefully before you buy your cage.

Top tip

Wooden cages are not ideal. Rats will eventually gnaw them to pieces. They are also difficult to keep clean as smelly **urine** soaks into the wood and makes it rotten.

Most rat cages have metal bars and a plastic base. Make sure the bars are narrow enough to stop a rat from squeezing through.

Top tip

Rats love to climb. Choose a cage that is tall enough to fit ramps, ladders, ropes, or branches inside so that your rats can exercise and play.

Choosing a tank

Another way of keeping rats is in a glass or **Plexiglas™** tank. However, it is very important to find a suitable lid for the tank. Choose one that lets in air but does not have large enough holes for your rats to climb through. It is very important to let enough air into the tank because otherwise **condensation** can collect on the inside of the tank walls, making it damp. This dampness can be dangerous to a rat's health.

Some cages are made entirely of metal. These can work well, as long as the floor is solid. Wire mesh floors are uncomfortable and can give rats sore feet.

Your rats will be happy to live in a Plexiglas™ tank like this. But be sure your pets have plenty of air and the tank has a tight-fitting lid so the rats cannot escape.

The perfect place

Once you have chosen a cage, you will need to find the right place for it. Rats can suffer from **heat stroke** if the temperature gets too high (over 68°F/20°C), so keep the cage out of direct sunlight and away from hot radiators. Rats can also become ill if they get too cold or are kept in a draft. Choose a sheltered place for the cage where they will not be too hot or too cold, and where there is not much change in temperature.

Keep your cage on a table or a shelf where the rats will not be bothered by other family pets.

Wood chips and shavings

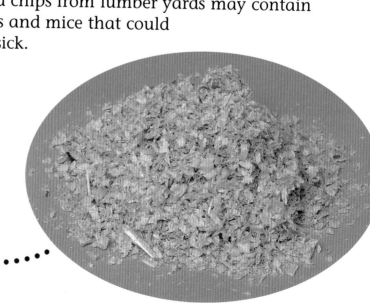

You will need something to cover the floor of the rats' cage. Wood chips and shavings are usually best. Make sure that you buy them from good pet stores rather than direct from a lumber yard. You do not want your wood chips and shavings to be full of nails, splinters, and other assorted trash. More seriously, wood chips from lumber yards may contain germs from wild rats and mice that could make your pet rats sick.

Wood chips and shavings should not be too fine or dusty—they could hurt a rat's eyes or get up its nose.

If good wood chips are hard to find, try using cat litter pellets made from recycled paper. Some rat owners prefer to use these.

Bedding

Rats need material to make themselves a bed. You can use shredded paper for bedding, but avoid newspaper as the ink is not good for rats. Paper towels are fine—let the rats do the tearing up. Hay is also suitable. This should always be bought from a pet store as hay straight from a farm may have fleas, **ticks,** or **mites** living in it.

Bedding boxes

You may want to make a bedding box for your rats. A plant pot stuffed with bedding is fine, and so is a cardboard shoebox with a rat-sized hole cut into its side. A bedding box will give your rats somewhere private to sleep. There are endless possibilities—you will find yourself looking at things and thinking, "I could give that to my rat to sleep in or play with."

You can make a simple bedding box from a cardboard shoebox filled with shredded paper.

19

Toys for rats

Rats are playful and curious creatures, so toys are a must. Your pets will enjoy having ladders and branches to climb on, shelves to run along, and tunnels to explore. Blocks of wood will give your rats something to chew on so they can keep their teeth short. Apple and pear wood are best. You can also buy chewing blocks from a pet store or rat **breeder.**

Blocks of wood are good for a rat's teeth and provide hours of chewing fun.

Climbing around

Many rat cages are fitted with shelves, ramps, and ladders, but you can also give your pets some branches to climb on. Choose rough branches that are still covered with bark, as these will help to keep rats' nails short.

Rats love climbing through, over, and under things!

Buying and making

Many pet stores and rat breeders sell colorful plastic tunnels, slides, and houses for rats to explore. You can also make your own rat toys from wide cardboard tubes and boxes with holes cut out of them. Try mixing up plastic toys with things you have made yourself to create an obstacle course. You could even try making a maze for your rats. Rats are so clever that they will soon find their way through the maze.

Your rats will have fun with almost anything you give them. But do not let your pets play with something they might swallow.

Not too full!

Do not fill the cage so full of toys that there is not enough room for a rat to run around. Most of all, rats enjoy plenty of open space.

No wheels

Exercise wheels are not good for rats. They are often too small for adult rats, especially for some of the larger **bucks.** Wheels with open bars can be dangerous as rats' tails can get caught up in the bars and injured. Solid wheels are usually made of plastic, and rats will chew on them. Many plastic wheels have dangerous metal spikes in the middle once the plastic coating is gone. It is much better for your rats to have other toys to play with and to have lots of exercise time outside their cage.

21

Looking After Your Rats

Your rat cage will need to be cleaned out thoroughly once a week. Throw out all the wood chips and bedding and wipe down the cage with a mild cleaner. You can buy safe cleaning sprays from a pet store. Do not forget to wipe down the shelves as well as any toys or branches in the cage. When everything is completely dry, put in fresh wood chips and bedding and put all the toys, branches, and shelves back inside the cage.

A weekly cleaning does not take long and will keep the cage smelling nice. Rat **urine** can become quite smelly, so you and your family will soon notice if you do not clean the cage regularly!

Top tip

You will not need to spend much time keeping your rats clean. Rats are very clean animals and they spend a lot of time **grooming** themselves. However, rats' tails can sometimes get grubby. You can clean them with mild soap and water. Just rub the tail gently with a cloth, then rinse it with clean water.

It is important to clean your rat cage every week. Otherwise, it will soon start to smell.

Daily cleaning

Besides giving the cage a weekly cleaning, you will also have some cleaning to do every day.

- Remove any uneaten food that is left scattered around the cage, especially fruits or vegetables that can attract flies.
- Wash the food bowl.
- Check the water bottle to make sure it is clean and full of fresh water.
- Remove any **feces** scattered inside the cage.
- Scoop out any wood chips made wet with urine.
- Rats can have an annoying habit of wetting their beds. Check that the bedding is clean and dry.

Washing is easiest if you have two bowls, side by side—one for washing and the other for rinsing.

Bath time

Occasionally your rats may need a bath. They will certainly need one if you decide to enter them for shows. If you treat your rats gently, bath times will be fun for all of you!

- Dip your rats into a bowl of lukewarm water and then hold them out of the water while you use a mild shampoo on their coats and tails. Be careful not to let any shampoo get into their eyes.
- Rinse your pets off in clean, warm water and dry them with a towel.
- Make sure your rats are completely dry and comfortable before they return to their cage.

After you have dried your rats, they may like to scamper around a bit to get warmed up.

23

Food for rats

A pet rats' basic diet should be a mixture of grains and cereals that you can buy from a pet store. Rat food is sold in boxes or packets, or even loose. However, make sure that the food is meant for rats. Gerbil and hamster food contains a lot of sunflower seeds and nuts that rats love, but they can cause sore spots on a rat's skin. It is much better to feed rats proper rat food, and give them an occasional sunflower seed or nut as a treat. Follow the feeding instructions on the package as a guideline to how much you should feed your pets.

Healthy extras

You can add a few extra **ingredients** to a rats' basic diet. Whole grain bread or toast, plain breakfast cereals, cooked rice or noodles, and cooked potato will all be appreciated by your pets— but don't overdo it! Your rats will also enjoy chewing on a dog biscuit. This is a tasty way to keep their teeth healthy.

You can buy rat food from a pet store. Make sure it is meant for rats.

Fruits and vegetables

Fruits and vegetables are good for rats.
- The best fruits are apples, although some rats love melon, cherries, and peaches. It is best to avoid very acidic fruits like oranges.
- Carrots, lettuce, cabbage, and celery are good vegetables to give your rats.
- Do not feed onions or very strong tasting vegetables to your pets. Start by giving your rats small amounts to see which kind of fruit or vegetable they prefer.

Feeding times

You can choose when to feed your rats, but it is usually best to feed them in the evening with a refill in the morning for breakfast if they need it. Rats will store extra food that they are not hungry enough to eat. Large stores mean that you are overfeeding them.

Most rats love nibbling on fresh fruits and vegetables.

Safety first

Rats can get upset stomachs from eating too many fruits or vegetables. Stick to very small amounts and only give your rats fruits or vegetables every other day.

Rats are enthusiastic eaters. They often climb right inside their feeding bowl.

25

Tasty treats

You can buy various treats for rats. These may be cereal bars that can be attached to the cage, tasty yogurt drops, or small cookies. Rats enjoy these, but you can offer them lots of other things, too. Rats will almost certainly enjoy a small taste of a cookie, chocolate, cake, or even ice cream—but do not give them too much. You know how bad it is to eat too much of these things, but rats do not. A tiny taste now and again is okay, but it is up to you not to let them get fat or sick by eating too many of the wrong foods.

Top tip

Usually, if you like eating something, your rats will probably like it too!

Your rats will probably love a small taste of ice cream, but never give them this much!

Pet stores sell a range of healthy treats for your rat like this one.

A bony treat!

A good, tasty treat for rats is a small bone with a little meat still on it. Rats enjoy meat, and chewing on the bone is good for their teeth. The bone can also provide valuable **calcium**, which will help your pets to have strong teeth and bones. A clean, cooked bone can be left in the cage for a day or two. But meaty bones must be removed after one day, as they will soon go bad and start to smell.

Water bottles

Finally, and most importantly, rats should always have fresh water to drink. A water bottle hung from the cage wires is best. You can also buy a clip to hang a water bottle from the lid of a tank. Water bottles work by letting drops of water flow whenever a rat licks the end of the spout. That way, pets can get enough to drink without the water dripping into the cage.

Vacations

Rats need daily care. If you are going away, make sure you have arranged for someone to look after your pets.

- Find a friend or neighbor who knows and likes rats.
- Ask them to visit your rats every day, to give them food and water, and clean out their cage.
- You should leave clear instructions about what to feed your pets and who to call if there is an emergency.

Rats need to drink lots of water. Remember to fill their bottle with new, fresh water every day.

Happy and healthy?

You need to check your pets regularly to make sure they are fit and well. Are your rats eating and drinking properly, and do they seem lively and **alert?** When you clean out the cage, check the rats' **feces.** They should not be very runny or too hard.

Daily checks

While you are handling your rats, feel them all over to make sure there are no lumps, bumps, or swellings on their bodies. Check that their coats are clean and soft, with no sore places or specks of dirt from fleas. Make sure that the skin on their ears and tails is clean and smooth, not rough and scaly.

Top tip

If you see something that could be a problem, tell your parents or another adult. They can help you decide whether you need to take your pet to the vet.

Feel each rat's body gently to make sure it has no fleas or **ticks** and no lumps or swellings.

Check that your rats' nails are not getting too long. You might need to have them trimmed.

Keep an eye on your pet's nails—they sometimes need trimming. Until you are used to rats, your veterinarian should do this for you. Also, check your pet's teeth. Rats' teeth keep growing all the time, and if your pets are not chewing enough, their teeth can become overgrown. If a rat's teeth become too long, they can stop it from eating properly.

This rat's teeth are the correct length. But if a rat is not chewing enough, its teeth might start growing too long. You will need to take your pet to the vet to have its teeth clipped.

Watch out!

When you are playing with your rats, watch for:

- How your rats move around. A limp or unusual way of walking may mean that your rat has been injured or is in pain.
- Weight change. Are your pets getting fatter or thinner? This can be a sign of a serious health problem.
- Head tilting. This may mean it has an ear problem.

Handling Your Rats

Pet rats are not wild animals. They have been **domesticated** so they are happy to live with people. But this does not mean you will be able to handle your rats immediately. As with every friendship, human or animal, it will take a little time to get to know each other and feel confident together.

Your rats will probably take a while to explore their new home and settle in comfortably.

A new home

When you first take your rats home, give them time to settle in before you try to play with them or handle them.

Some rats settle in quicker than others. Some will be standing up at the bars demanding your attention as soon as they have explored their cage. Others will be shy and will have to be coaxed out of their cage. Food is always a great way to make friends. Offer some food and let the rat take it from your fingers. If you have a very shy rat, you may need to put a morsel near the front of the cage and sit quietly while the rat gathers the courage to eat it.

Top tip

Do not try to pick up your pets immediately. Remember that your hand will look enormous to a rat. The rat has to learn that you will not hurt it.

Easy does it

Take some time to allow your rats to get used to your voice and your hands. Your pets will have had a lot of changes in their short lives, and they will need to feel confident. Soon they will be taking food from you, first through the bars of their cage and then directly from your hand. They may even start putting their feet on the palm of your hand while they take their food. This sort of confidence means that a rat is ready to be handled.

You will seem giant to your rats. Talk to them softly and let them get used to the sound of your voice.

Soon, your rats will be happy to take food from your hand.

Other pets

- You will need to be very careful about letting rats meet other pets. Most cats and dogs could kill a rat if they wanted to. Take care when you introduce them and never leave them alone together.
- Rats can also frighten or even kill some other pets. Do not let them near hamsters or gerbils, even in separate cages. It may be too upsetting for the smaller animal.

31

Picking up your rat

Never pick up a rat by its tail. This is very frightening for your pet and may even injure it. Pick up a rat by putting one hand over its back and scooping it up into your other hand. This means that it will be sitting on one of your hands with your other hand over it. Pet it and speak softly to it. Try not to do anything too suddenly.

At first, a rat may not seem to like being handled. But it is important to hold it as much as you can so that it gets used to being held. If the rat needs to be stopped from jumping or falling, you can steady it by holding the very base of its tail next to its bottom.

Offer a treat, such as a trickle of ice cream, on your fingers. Your pet will soon learn that handling means nice things are going to happen!

Pick up a rat by putting one hand on its back and scooping it up with your other hand.

A rat will like being held against your body while you support its bottom with your other hand.

32

Top tip

If your rats try to hide in your clothing, let them! Rats love being carried around in their owner's pockets or T-shirt. It can be a good way of getting your pets used to riding around on you.

Contented chuckles

As your rats become more confident, let them sit on your shoulder. This is a favorite place for many rats, and they will happily sit with you while you watch TV or walk around the house. Often a happy rat will "chuckle" and make a tooth-grinding noise that can sound quite loud when it is right in your ear! Some rats even lick their owner's face. They have very soft, velvety tongues and very tickly whiskers.

Playtime

Try to set aside some time every day for your pets to play outside their cage. It is best to keep your rats in just one or two rooms, where you can stay with them and make sure that they do not get into any trouble. You can give your pets some tubes and boxes to play in, but they will mainly enjoy just being out and exploring.

Top tip

You should always remember to wash your hands after handling a rat.

Your rats will love to run along the backs of sofas and chairs to inspect whoever is sitting there!

Rat-proofing a room

Before you let your rats out to play, you will need to make sure that they cannot get hurt. You will also have to keep things safe from your rats. Be careful that there is nothing in their reach that they can chew to bits.

Inspect the room for any places where a rat could get stuck or lost. The best way to do this is to pretend to be a rat. Lie down flat on the floor and ask yourself what you can see that is rat-sized and might seem worth exploring. Look for gaps in fireplaces and behind cabinets, or cracks in floorboards. These will all need to be blocked up. Check also that your pets cannot get inside furniture. A number of pet rats meet a sudden death by being sat on in sofas or chairs.

Electricity alert

Rats love chewing things. Electrical cords and TV, video, and computer wires all look like tasty things for a rat to chew on. This could be very dangerous for your pet because it might get an electric shock that could kill it. If there are some cords that cannot be moved, fit protective sleeves around them to stop them from being chewed.

Before you let your rats out to play, make sure there are no electrical cords lying around.

Chewing trouble

Rats can be quite destructive if they are not watched. A favorite trick is to chew any material they can reach from their cage. So do not leave your best clothing near your pets' cage. They may reach out and drag it in. And if a rat disappears behind the curtains when it is out playing, it may well be chewing holes in them!

If you leave anything close to the cage, the rats will try to find a way of dragging it inside.

Top tips

- Rats often steal things. This can be amusing, but rats are not clever enough to know when something is really harmful.
- Check your room to see what is lying around and remove any objects that would be bad for a rat to chew on.

Rats are interested in objects they can pick up and carry. Key rings, candy wrappers, pens, and even jewelry may all find their way into a rat's hiding place!

35

Some Health Problems

Rats are quite healthy little animals, but there are a few illnesses and problems that rat owners need to recognize. Because rats are very small, they can get ill very fast. Having an experienced veterinarian is important.

Colds

Runny eyes and nose, wheezing, and sneezing may mean your rat has a cold. Rats can catch colds if they are in a draft, if the temperature drops dramatically, or if they are near another rat with a cold. Sometimes the liquid coming from your rat's eyes and nose may be pink and look like blood, but it is not. Colds can be very serious to rats, so take your pet to the vet. The vet will give your pet an **antibiotic** shot to help fight the cold. You must also keep it away from other rats to stop them from catching the cold, too. Make sure your rat is warm and drinking lots of water.

If your rat becomes seriously ill, take it to the vet as soon as possible.

Skin problems

Spots and sores on a rat's skin can be painful and itchy. There are two main causes of skin problems in rats. The first cause is diet. Your rat may have been eating too many sunflower seeds or nuts. If this is the case, replace its normal diet for a few days with plain food, such as boiled rice and plain bread. If your rat's skin starts to look better, then diet was probably the cause.

The second cause of sores, scabs, and bald patches are **mites.** These are tiny **parasites** that live in some animals' coats. They may have come from hay or straw or from another rat. If you have recently bought a new rat, you should ask your vet to check it for mites. Your vet will give you a special shampoo to kill the mites. Change all the bedding and wood chips in your pet's cage and do not let it near other rats until it is clear of mites.

Tummy troubles

- **Diarrhea** is often caused by too much fruit, too many vegetables, or too many unhealthy treats. This is easily corrected. Just feed your rat a very plain diet for a few days.
- Sometimes, a rat can develop diarrhea if it is traveling or being moved from place to place. This normally settles down on its own.
- If your rat is suffering from **constipation,** it will have very hard **feces** that are difficult to pass. Constipation can be very painful. It is often caused by too much dry food. Feeding your rat a little lettuce or salad greens can improve things.

Normal rat **feces** should be soft and **cylindrical** in shape. If they are runny or very dry, your rat has a problem.

37

Ear problems

If your rat starts to hold its head tilted to one side, there is probably something wrong with its ears. Your rat may even have trouble balancing. Your vet will give you some ear drops to help clear the **infection.** Rats usually recover well, although some bad ear infections may leave a rat with a permanently tilted head.

Lumps and bumps

Many rats develop lumps and bumps. Sometimes these may be soft and full of **pus.** These are called **abscesses** and are caused by an infection developing around a wound or a bite. Abscesses can be drained and cleaned and usually heal very well.

Your vet will be able to give you advice about what to look for when examining your rats at home.

Other lumps may be harder masses of fatty skin. Most of these lumps are **benign,** which means they are harmless. They can often be removed by an operation. Sadly, rats sometimes develop **cancerous tumors.** These are often just like the benign fatty lumps, but they feel harder. They grow fast and eventually make the rat very sick. If this happens, you should talk to your veterinarian about whether it would be best to have your rat put to sleep.

Eye problems

- If your rat has watery or runny eyes, ask an adult to help you bathe it with a soft cloth soaked in warm water. There may be a piece of dust in your rat's eye.
- If the problem comes back after bathing the eyes, it could be an infection. You will need to take your rat to the vet for some **antibiotics.**

Teeth problems

A rat's teeth continue growing throughout its life, so your pets will need lots of hard things to gnaw on to wear down their teeth. Sometimes, a rat's teeth can grow so long that it cannot eat properly and starts to lose weight. If this happens, your vet can clip your rat's teeth to the right length. Your rat will not like this, but it will not hurt.

Top tip

Make sure you give your pets lots of hard blocks of wood and other things to chew on to keep their teeth the right length.

A rat's teeth keep growing all the time. This rat has lost one of its upper teeth so its lower tooth has not worn down. It has grown extremely long.

Too hot

If the cage is left in direct sunlight or too close to a hot radiator, your pets may become overheated and suffer from **heat stroke.** They will look uncomfortable and their breathing will become rapid and shallow. Quickly move the cage to cooler surroundings and encourage your rats to drink cool water. If your rats collapse, wrap them in cool—not ice cold—damp towels and take them to the veterinarian.

Too cold

If your rats become really cold, they may suffer from **hypothermia.** They will seem very slow and sluggish and may even collapse. Their bodies will be hunched up and feel cold to the touch. The best thing to do is to hold your pets inside your shirt so your body temperature heats them up gently. If your rats do not show signs of getting better within ten minutes, take them to the vet.

Top tip

If a rat becomes too cold, a little drink of warm milk or water will help to increase its body temperature.

If a rat develops hypothermia, you need to act fast. You could try taking it to a warm place and wrapping it up in a towel or blanket.

40

Danger signs

Watch out for these danger signs. They might mean that a rat is very ill.

- Your rat is sitting hunched up as if it is very uncomfortable. Its eyes may be half closed or it may be trembling. Its coat may look scruffy because it is not **grooming** itself.
- Your rat cannot walk without falling over. It may have a severe ear **infection.**
- Your rat has difficulty breathing, and is gasping and wheezing. This may mean that the rat has **pneumonia.**

If your rat has any of these signs, you should contact your veterinarian immediately.

If your rat is looking more scruffy than normal, it may be a sign that your pet is sick.

Accidents can happen

Sometimes rats get broken legs. If this happens, you will need to immediately take your pet to a vet. The vet will decide whether an operation is necessary to help heal the leg. Sometimes it may be necessary to **amputate** a leg. Rats cope surprisingly well with only three legs. Occasionally a rat may have to be put to sleep if its injuries are too serious.

In spite of these possible illnesses, you will probably find that your rats are healthy and active for most of their lives. However, a rat's life is short—only about two and a half years—so it will not be long before you have to think about your rat as an old animal.

Growing Old

Old rats need special care. They feel the cold more and are less active and **agile** than younger rats. It is a good idea to remove any ladders and climbing toys from their cage, as their balance may not be very good.

Give an old rat a quiet life with lots of gentle care and affection. It will still have a lot to enjoy, even if it is not as lively as it used to be. Even though it is old and slow, your rat will still be a friend who likes to sit on your shoulder.

Once a rat is over two years old, it will probably start to look old.

A peaceful end

Some old rats die peacefully in their sleep without ever becoming really sick. Others get lots of little illnesses, aches, and pains. These can mean that an old rat's life is no longer very enjoyable.

If your rat is sick and near the end of its life, you may decide that it is a good idea to talk to your vet about having it put to sleep. To put your rat to sleep, the vet will give it a shot. The shot does not hurt—it just makes your pet feel sleepy. Before you can count to ten, your rat will be asleep for the last time.

Saying goodbye

It is hard to lose a pet that you have loved. It can seem very unfair that your rat has lived for such a short time. However, there are some things that you need to remember.

It can help to have a special burial place for your pet. You could plant a flower or a shrub on it.

- It is not your fault, or the vet's fault, that your pet has died. It is just a fact that rats do not live long.
- When a pet dies, it is perfectly normal for people-adults as well as children-to cry for a while.
- Eventually the pain will pass and you will be left with happy memories of your pet. Maybe you will think about having another rat to look after and enjoy.

Keeping a Record

It is fun to keep a record of your pet rats. Buy a big scrapbook and fill it with notes and photos. Then you can look back at it and remind yourself of all the things you and your pets did together. Your rat scrapbook can also include general information about rats and how to care for them.

A special diary

Begin your scrapbook when you first get your pet. You could start with the very first photo taken of your rats when they came to live with you. Were they really those tiny kittens? Or what about the first time you held them? Or when they first sat on your shoulder? Or when Mom or Grandma was brave enough to hold them?

You can write down special events in the lives of your pets, such as the first time they explored your room or the first time you gave them a bath. You can also make a note of the funny things your rats do when they are eating or playing.

Choosing which pictures to put in your scrapbook can be a lot of fun. Maybe you could ask other people which ones they like best, too.

Useful information

You can collect articles and information about rats and rat care and stick them into your scrapbook. They will soon build up into a good store of tips and guidance. You can also keep lists of your friends and contacts in rat clubs, the dates of shows, and useful websites about rats and how to look after them.

Rat shows

You may decide to show your rats. Societies such as the American Fancy Rat and Mouse Association have junior memberships and junior classes at shows. Maybe your rats will win ribbons that you can keep in your scrapbook!

When you have finished adding pictures to your scrapbook, it may be a good idea to label them. Otherwise, in years to come, you may forget what each picture is showing.

Your scrapbook will help to make sure that you never forget the special times that you and your rats enjoyed together.

45

Glossary

abscess   soft lump filled with pus

agile   able to move quickly and easily

alert   lively and interested in everything

amputate   surgically remove a leg or an arm

antibiotic   medicine that fights infection

benign   harmless or not dangerous

breed   mate and then give birth to young

breeder   someone who keeps animals and encourages them to mate and produce young

buck   male rat

calcium   substance that is good for building strong teeth and bones

cancerous   caused by cancer. Cancer is a disease that destroys the body's healthy cells.

condensation   water that collects as drops on a cold surface

constipation   problem caused by hard feces that makes it difficult to pass a bowel movement

cylindrical   shaped like a tube

diarrhea   runny feces

doe   female rat

domesticate   to tame an animal so that it can live with humans

fancy rat   rat with special markings or colors, recognized as a particular type by rat societies

feces   solid waste matter passed out of the body

gregarious   sociable, or fond of company

groom   clean an animal's coat. Animals often groom themselves.

heat stroke   illness caused by getting too hot

hypothermia   illness caused by getting too cold

illegal   against the law

infection   illness that makes part of the body fill with pus

ingredient   part of a food or meal

kitten   baby rat

litter   number of baby rats born together

mammal   animal with fur or hair on its body that feeds its babies with milk

mite   small creature that lives on another animal's skin and sucks its blood

nocturnal   active at night

parasite   small creature, like a flea, tick, or worm, that lives on or inside another animal

pest   creature that causes problems for people, often by carrying diseases

Plexiglas™   clear, strong plastic

pneumonia   illness where the lungs become infected and fill with fluid

pus   thick yellow fluid inside an infected part of the body

rodent   animal with strong front teeth for gnawing

scavenge   hunt for food

tick   small creature that lives on another animal's skin and sucks its blood

tumor   lump or growth

urine   liquid passed out of the body containing water and waste substances

vermin   animals that are pests, such as wild rats and mice

warm-blooded   used to describe an animal that can keep its body at the same temperature

Further Reading

Bulla, Gisela. *Fancy Rats.* Hauppauge, N.Y.: Barron's Educational Series, Incorporated, 1999.

Buscis, Gerry and Barbara Somerville. *Training Your Pet Rat.* Hauppauge, N.Y.: Barron's Educational Series, Incorporated, 2000.

Conniff, Richard. *Rats!* New York: Random House, Incorporated, 2002.

Erlbach, Arlene. *My Pet Rat.* Minneapolis: Lerner Publishing Group, 1998.

Grolier Educational Staff. *Rats.* Danbury, Conn.: Grolier Educational, 2001.

Useful Addresses

Rat and Mouse Club of America
13075 Springdale St. PMB 302
Westminster, CA 92683
http://www.rmca.org

National Alternative Pet Association
P.O. Box 369
Burnet, TX 78611
http://www.altpet.net/

The American Society for the Prevention of Cruelty to Animals
424 E. 92nd St.
New York, NY 10128
Tel: (212) 876-7700
http://www.aspca.org

Disclaimer
All Internet addresses (URLs) given in this book were valid at the time of going to press. However, due to the dynamic nature of the Internet, some addresses may have changed, or sites may have ceased to exist since publication. While the author and publisher regret any inconvenience this may cause readers, no responsibility for any such changes can be accepted by either the author or the publisher.

Index